The Burnt Stick

The Burnt Stick

by Anthony Hill

illustrated by Mark Sofilas

Houghton Mifflin Company

BOSTON · NEW YORK 1995

The aboriginal stories mentioned are told in *The Story of Crow,* by Pat Torres and Magdalene Williams, and *Story About Feeling,* by Bill Neidjie, both published by Magabala Books, Broome, Australia.

First American edition 1995 by
Houghton Mifflin Company

First published in Australia by Penguin Books
Australia Ltd., 1994

Manufactured in the United States of America

Typography by David Saylor
The text of this book is set in 14-point Arrus.
The illustrations are charcoal-pencil drawings reproduced as halftones.

KPT   10   9   8   7   6   5   4   3   2   1

Library of Congress Cataloging-in-Publication Data
Hill, Anthony.
The burnt stick / by Anthony Hill : illustrated by Mark Sofilas.—1st American ed.   p.   cm.
Summary: Growing up in a missionary home run by white men, John Jagamarra, who is part aborigine and part white, misses the mother from whom he's been separated and the culture of his own people.
ISBN 0-395-73974-8
1. Australian aborigines—Juvenile fiction.
[1. Australian aborigines—Fiction.
2. Australia—Fiction.   3. Mothers and sons—Fiction.   4. Missions—Australia—Fiction.]
I. Sofilas, Mark, ill.   II. Title.
PZ7.H5475Bu   1995
[Fic]—dc20   95-2698   CIP   AC

To Vanessa

—A. H.

To my father

—M. S.

Although the incidents described in this story are mostly fictional, they are based on a central fact. It was the practice of the authorities in many parts of Australia, until as late as the 1960s, to take aboriginal children of mixed parentage away from their mothers, and to have them brought up either in institutions or with foster parents.

—Anthony Hill,
Canberra, Australia, 1994

The Burnt Stick

John Jagamarra grew up at the Pearl Bay Mission for Aboriginal Children on the coast in the far northwest of Australia. It was a very beautiful place. The palm trees and the scented vines grew down to the slow green tropical sea, where the children used to fish and dive for shells. But it was not home.

The mission had been built many years ago by the Fathers. Mostly they were good men. They built a stone church—with a bell tower and narrow windows with yellow glass—like the ones they remembered from their own country on the other side of the world. They read from the Bible of a loving God, and sang the Latin Mass every Sunday, the aboriginal altar boys in white surplices.

The Fathers built a school of corrugated iron painted gray, with sleeping huts (four boys or girls to a room) and outbuildings—the dairy, bakery, and machinery shed. They planted a vegetable garden that grew almost anything, beans and peanuts and ripe crimson watermelons; and an orchard heavy with fruit, mangoes and pawpaws and sweet bananas.

They taught the aboriginal children how to read and write in English, how to add and subtract, and how to recite the catechism. They taught them how to grow crops, how to thresh the rice at harvest, how to bake bread, and how to milk the goats.

They taught the girls how to cook and to sew cotton dresses, and the boys, like John Jagamarra, how to make bricks in the kiln, how to plane wood, and how to make things in the carpenter's shop. Still, it was not like home.

For the Fathers did not teach the children the songs, the dancing, and the picture making of their own people. They did not speak to them, as their families did, in the aboriginal tongues or tell them the stories of the Dreaming and the Ancestor spirits of the land that once had been told around the campfires. They did not show them how to follow the kangaroo through the bush, or how to make spears, or how to find where the wild yams grew. These things the Fathers did not know, and so they were not allowed. And, as the years went by, most people forgot them.

No, it was not like home.

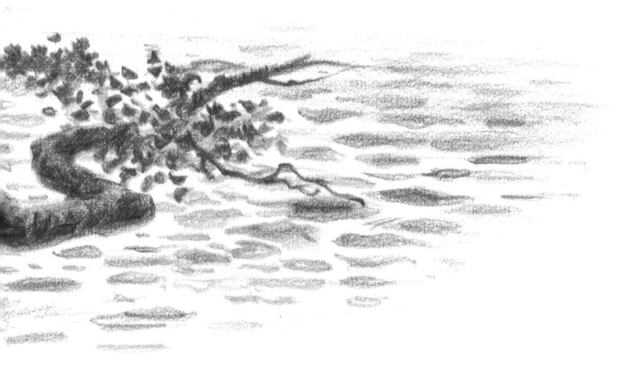

It was not like home because very few of the children had been born at Pearl Bay Mission. Nor were their families there, and they rarely came to visit. It was a long way, and often they were not permitted. Most of the children, like John Jagamarra, had been taken from their mothers when they were very young, and sent by the government men from the Welfare Department to the Fathers at places like Pearl Bay. That was the law of the white people at the time, though it is different now.

The Welfare said it was for the children's own good. After all, their fathers were generally white men—sometimes stockmen, or cooks, or overseers at the inland cattle stations. It was felt to be best if those children with light-colored skin were sent to be taught in the white man's way.

No one asked the mothers before the children were taken away. Even if they had, it would have made no difference. The Welfare believed the mothers would soon get over their loss. And no one asked the children—they would soon forget. Yet John Jagamarra did not forget. He was nearly five when the Big Man from Welfare came looking for him—and you can remember many things when you are almost five years old.

Growing up by the pearl-shining sea, John Jagamarra remembered the heat and the dust, the low scrub and the red horizons of the inland desert country near Dryborough Station where he had been born. He remembered the pool in the creek bed where he and the others would swim naked after rain, and the flat lizard rock where they would lie afterward, sunning themselves.

Sitting through the long afternoons in the schoolroom, sweaty in the shirts and trousers

the Fathers said the boys must wear (though, mercifully, never shoes), John Jagamarra would remember the camp under the acacia trees, just down the track from the station homestead. He would remember the dogs stretched asleep in the shade, pink tongues hanging out; the sounds of women talking beneath the tin-and-bough shelters; and the sharp cries of excitement when the men rode in on their horses from a day of rounding up the long-horned cattle.

But it was at night, lying awake and lonely in his narrow iron bed at the mission, that he could remember things most clearly. It was then that he could feel the cool desert night embracing him, folded in his mother's arms by the campfire after they had eaten—lying there contented, half asleep, sensing her presence and the touch of her skin, the color of evening, so much darker than his own.

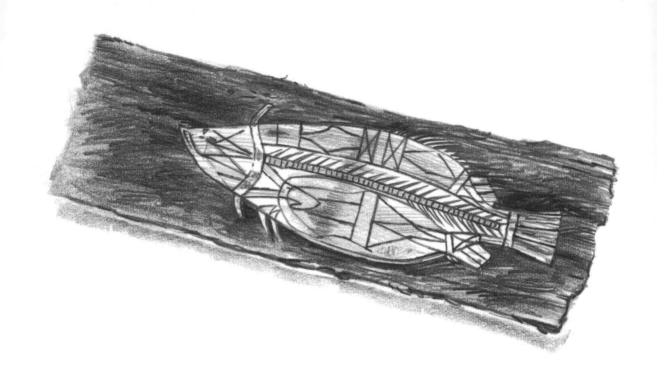

John did not know who his father was. He was a white man, a traveler who had come to Dryborough Station some years ago, the people said, and then had gone. But it did not matter all that much. Within the camp, John felt membership in a larger family, each one of whom looked on him as part of their own. There were ties of blood and country through his mother and grandmother and his cousins. There were ties with those who belonged with him to *Barramundi*, the great fish, that Ancestor

They would tell of what had happened during the day, whom they had seen, and what they had been told. Sometimes the women who worked at the house would laugh at Mrs. Grainger, the boss's wife, complaining of dust in the homestead, and the cook getting mad at a fly in the kitchen. Mrs. Grainger was a sensible woman whom the camp trusted, and the cook knew his job—but they never seemed able to accept that there would *always* be dust and flies, whatever you did.

spirit into whose Dreaming he would be initi-
ated when he became a man.

It would be a long time yet before he began
to learn the law—the aboriginal lore—of his
people, and the secrets of the land. For the pre-
sent, it was enough just to *be*: to watch the play
of firelight in the night embers, smell the scent
of wood smoke and tobacco, listen to the voice
of the older people as they spoke among themselves around the camp.

Sometimes the men would tell of the horse-breaking or the country through which they had ridden; of the rocks, the water holes, and those places that had meaning in the stories of the land they knew. And sometimes, because the children were there, they would sing these stories and dance—with the women beating time on their clapping sticks. Stories of a past long gone and yet, strangely, still with them. Of the Crow and the Eagle and how they were always fighting between themselves. Of the King Brown Snake, whose pink eye could still be

seen watching at night among the stars. Of how the Frill-Necked Lizard, who once had been a smooth and handsome creature, was made by the Creator to look so ugly because he had broken the law.

At these times, John Jagamarra remembered how he would nestle deeper into his mother's arms, and laugh with pleasure, and feel as if the life of the camp beneath the trees on Dryborough Station could go on forever.

Yet nothing goes on forever.

One night, when the young moon had risen and they were sitting around the fire, Charlie Warragin, the head stockman, looked at John's mother and said, "Liyan, I have heard they are coming to take away your son in the morning."

John Jagamarra felt his mother become very tense, her fear flowing into himself. She held him tighter in her arms and cried, "Who is coming to take him away? Where will they take him?"

"The Big Man from Welfare," said Charlie Warragin. "I have heard he is traveling with the police truck to all the camps in this part of the country and taking the light-skinned ones to the Fathers at Pearl Bay. He was with the mob at Richmond Downs the day before yesterday. He will be here tomorrow."

"When will they bring my son back to me?"

"He will not be coming back," said Charlie Warragin. And the old man Jabal, who knew much and taught the law to the young men, agreed. "They will bring him up in the ways of the white man. It will be many years before he

can return, and his life will never be the same."

"They cannot do this thing!" cried Liyan.

"They can, and they will. It is the law of the white man that says so."

"I will tell the boss, tell Mrs. Grainger. She will stop them."

"She will be able to do nothing."

"I love my son! This is his family! They cannot come to take him away!"

"They have been coming from the day he was born," said Jabal.

John Jagamarra heard his mother begin to weep, and he cried with her though he did not fully understand. She picked him up, and held him close to her breast, and rocked him as she had when he was a baby. She wept with a low, wordless sound, and he felt the wet tears on his naked skin.

"I will run with him into the desert country and we will hide from the Big Man."

"There is nowhere safe to run," said Charlie Warragin, "and in the end they will find him."

When he finished speaking, John's grandmother and all the other women in the camp began to moan and cry with grief, as they did

when one of the people died and their spirit returned to the Ancestors. They beat the ground, and threw dust over themselves, and mourned for the loss of one of their own.

The grieving went on late into the night. The fire had burnt to ashes and the young moon had almost finished his journey across the sky before the camp lay down to sleep. But Liyan did not rest that night. Her son slept against her breast, yet she sat awake through the hours wondering what she could do to stop the Big Man from taking John and sending him to the Fathers at Pearl Bay Mission.

And then an idea came to her.

V*ery early,* when the first splinter of light appeared in the eastern sky and before the dawn birds had started singing, Liyan woke her boy. "Come," she said, "there is something we can do."

They went to the campfire where the cinders were cold. Liyan took a stick that had burnt black, almost to charcoal. She ground the soot and the charred ends of the stick into a powder in the palm of her hand, and began to rub it into John Jagamarra's skin.

She rubbed it into his feet and up his legs and all along his back. She rubbed it over his belly and chest. She rubbed it into his hands and along his arms. She rubbed it on his neck, and over his face, and into the strands of his brown hair. So that when the rest of the camp woke up that morning, John Jagamarra had been changed. His light-brown skin was now as dark as the others—and how they laughed when they saw him, and said what a clever thing Liyan had done.

"I would not have thought of that," remarked the old man Jabal.

But Charlie Warragin asked, "Will it be enough to trick the Big Man from Welfare?"

"Oh yes," said John Jagamarra's grandmother. "Even I might not have known him unless I looked closely—and as for the white men, we all look much the same to them."

That morning, when the sun had risen, the men and the older children left the camp: some to the stockyards, some into the back country where they could not be asked questions. Only the women and the youngest children were left at the camp under the acacia trees. And there they were, sitting silently, when the Big Man drove the truck down the track from the station homestead. There were two policemen as well, and the boss's wife, Mrs. Grainger, sitting between them.

The truck had a kind of wire cage on the back, with a gate that padlocked and canvas shades that rolled down if the sun got too hot, or if they didn't want you to see if anyone was locked inside.

They got out and stood uncomfortably on the other side of the campfire. The two policemen and Harriet Grainger did not like what they were going to do. But it was the law.

"Which one is Liyan?" asked the Big Man from Welfare. He was a tall man, with freckles and sandy hair and pale blue watercolored eyes, squinting in the morning sun.

"I bin Liyan, boss," said John Jagamarra's mother softly, in the shy pidgin English with which her people mocked the white man's speech.

"I am told you have a son," said the Big Man, "who must come with me to Pearl Bay."

"Why, boss?"

"Because he must be taught the white man's way, to read and write in English, to count, and to learn a trade. The blackfeller's way is not enough for him. You know that. It is the same for all those with light-colored skin."

"But my boy does not have light-colored skin, boss."

"I have been told differently."

The Big Man from Welfare was beginning to sound impatient and the sun was hurting his eyes. "Isn't that so, Mrs. Grainger?" He looked to the boss's wife, standing there twisting her wedding ring and wishing she were anywhere else.

"Oh, Liyan," said Harriet Grainger. "I'm sorry. It's not right. But there was nothing I could do."

"That's okay, missus," said Liyan. "We're all blackfellers in this mob. Isn't that so? Do you want to see, boss?"

"Show me," said the man from Welfare. He was irritated. It was a long way to come for nothing, and he had much farther to go.

John Jagamarra stood up next to his mother, the sun behind him. His skin, where Liyan had rubbed it with the burnt stick, was the color of earth when a shadow falls on it. But she was careful not to touch him, as she ached to do, in case the charcoal brushed away, showing the light-brown flesh underneath.

No one said a thing. Even Mrs. Grainger was

silent as the Big Man walked across to the boy and his mother, and stood looking down at them. The sun shone directly into his water-rinsed eyes, for the women had placed themselves carefully. He looked from one to the other for a very long time.

"Is this your son?" he asked at last.

"Yes, boss," answered Liyan.

"Is it?" He turned angrily to Mrs. Grainger.

"That is John Jagamarra," the woman replied uneasily.

"Then there has been a mistake. I have been wasting my time." And without speaking another word, the Big Man from Welfare and the two policemen who were with him got into the truck and drove away.

There was much laughter and clapping of hands in the camp when they had gone. The women ran up to Liyan and John Jagamarra, and hugged them. They said what a smart trick it was that had been played on the Big Man, and how proud the men would be when they heard of its success. The children ran down to the water hole to swim and to wash away the charcoal from John Jagamarra's body.

Only Mrs. Grainger, who had stayed behind, seemed doubtful. "It *was* a clever thing to do," she said, "and it shows how much you love your son. But, Liyan, was it wise? Don't you think

34

the men from government will hear of it and come back one day?"

"Who's going to tell them, missus? Not us."

"Nor I," said Harriet Grainger. "But they have their books and their papers and ways of finding things out. And if that happens, won't it be worse for you and your boy?"

"Ah," replied Liyan, "do not worry yourself, missus. If the Big Man comes back, I will use the burnt stick once again."

"It may not work a second time," said Harriet Grainger.

The same warning was given by Jabal that

evening around the campfire. He was as pleased as any of them that the Big Man had not known John Jagamarra. But he said, "They do not like to be laughed at, these men from government. When the Big Man hears that you have made a fool of him, he will be angry and will surely return. It would be wise if we were cautious and listened to everything that is said."

For a while it seemed unnecessary. The weeks went by without any news of the Big Man. Until, one evening, Charlie Warragin said he had heard that the man from Welfare was on his way again to Dryborough Station.

"He will be here by morning," said Charlie Warragin.

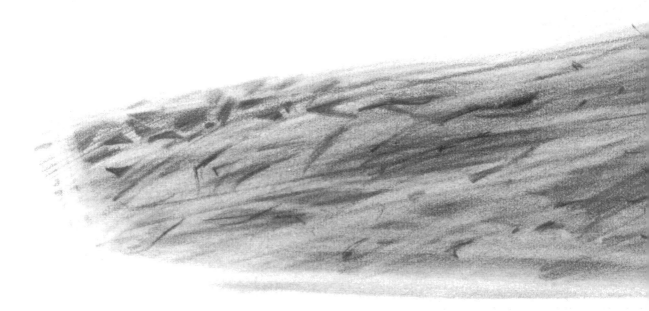

That night the women did not mourn for the coming of day. They knew what must be done. Before the morning star had faded and the first birds started to sing, they were awake. And, each taking a stick that had been burnt in the campfire, they again rubbed the charcoal into John Jagamarra's body, just as his mother had done. They rubbed him until he was as dark as the coal-black embers—as dark as themselves. So that when the Big Man from Welfare arrived that morning and stood looking at John Jagamarra, once more he could not tell him apart from the others.

"I do not understand this," he said to Liyan. "I have been told that his father was a white man and that he must come with me to Pearl Bay Mission. It is written on my papers. But his skin is as dark as your own."

"Yes, boss," said Liyan. "Dark as a burnt stick."

"You are not pretending?" exclaimed the Big Man, sounding stern and important.

"I am not pretending anything," said Liyan,

"What's this?" the Big Man asked, with an edge of suspicion in his voice.

Everyone was silent, holding their breaths, as Liyan again gazed at him and said calmly, "It's ashes from the fire, boss. He was playing in them this morning. You know what blackfellers are like. We always bin sitting in the dust."

And she laughed. They all laughed. Even the policemen and the Big Man found themselves beginning to smile. But there was a doubt behind the dark, laughing eyes. Liyan had not told

looking him full in the face until he had to turn his pale weeping eyes away from the sun. "The papers might be wrong. What you see is what you see."

"My papers have never been wrong before," said the tall sandy man. And he patted John Jagamarra on the head.

It was enough to make some of the soot from the boy's hair brush onto the Big Man's fingers, and he saw at once the dark stains on his hands.

a lie, but would the government men guess at the greater truth her words suggested?

There was a long silence, during which even the air seemed not to move. At last the Big Man, wiping his hands, said, "Very well."

And for the second time he drove away. For the second time there was laughter in the camp. For the second time the women told themselves how clever they had been, and admired Liyan's daring at mentioning the ashes. She would do anything to keep her son. Once more, the

children went to the water hole to swim and to wash away the charcoal from John Jagamarra's brown skin.

That night there was much singing and dancing under the acacia trees. Even Jabal seemed half-satisfied. He sang the story of Crow, who some call *Wangkid*, and of how he once had been a bird as white as the cockatoos. But one day he swallowed a burning coal that had been dropped from the sky by his rival, the Eagle, and his feathers had been scorched by the fire.

"That is why," said Jabal, as he finished his song, "the Crow has been black from that day to this. As the color of Crow was changed by the

fire, so was the skin of John Jagamarra changed with the help of a burnt stick." And then he added, "There is more than one meaning to any story. Never forget that Crow is the most cunning of birds, and will always think of another trick of his own to play upon the Eagle. So with the Big Man from Welfare. This is not over yet."

But Charlie Warragin said that the Big Man would surely not return. Even if he did, they could always deceive him with the help of a burnt stick for yet a third time.

They should have listened to Jabal, who was wise and knew many things.

That night the camp went to sleep under the stars and the watching pink eye of the King Brown Snake. They slept soundly, having eaten much and danced even more, and no one was awake to see the thin edge of dawn slip beneath the eastern horizon. No one saw the morning star fade, or heard the first birds sing.

And no one heard the truck with a cage on the back coming slowly down the track from the homestead, its lights turned off and the engine running quietly. No one saw it stop, and the Big Man and the two policemen get out, and walk softly across to the sleeping camp.

No one knew anything until one of the dogs woke and began to bark at the strangers. But by then it was too late. By then the Big Man was standing over Liyan and John Jagamarra asleep by her side. By then he had seen that the boy's skin was not like his mother's, the color of evening, but was soft light-brown like the earth in the early sunrise.

"You thought you could trick me," said the Big Man from Welfare. "But I know a better trick than that. I spoke to the boss this time—not his missus—and waited where you could not see me. Now I have come back and this time your boy must come with me."

Liyan jumped up from the ground where she had been lying and took John Jagamarra in her arms.

"No!" she cried. "You cannot take him! I love him! He is my son!"

"It is the law," said the Big Man, "and I must. He will be taught the white man's ways. And you can come to see him sometimes."

"It is too far to walk to the Fathers at Pearl Bay Mission."

"That cannot be helped. It is for the best."

The whole camp was awake, crying that the men from government could not take John Jagamarra from them. He had been born at Dryborough Station and was one of their own. But the Big Man from Welfare said that he could—and he did. He snatched John Jagamarra, terrified, from his mother's arms; and as she and the boy cried for each other, and the whole camp screamed in anger and dismay, the Big Man walked to the truck and got inside the cabin. There was no need to put the boy in the cage on the back. He was small, and there was only one of him.

John Jagamarra struggled and wept for his mother, but the Big Man held him tightly and would not let go.

"No! No!" shrieked Liyan and all the people. "Give me back my boy. Give back John Jagamarra. He is part of us!"

They held on to the side of the truck and beat the panels of the doors. But the policemen with batons stopped them from trying to seize the boy, and the people could not stop the heavy truck as it moved off down the track and began the long journey to Pearl Bay Mission.

"Mother!" cried John Jagamarra. "I want my mother."

And the last thing that John Jagamarra saw through his frightened eyes, as he looked through the window, was the sight of his mother clinging to the door handle, pleading, and trying to run with the truck as she was dragged through the dust. Until, at last, she could hold on no longer and fell face down into the dirt.

"It is hard, but she will soon get over it," said the Big Man to Mrs. Grainger, when he passed her homestead. She had come onto the veranda, for her husband had told her what was going to happen. "They are not like us. They soon forget."

But John Jagamarra did not forget. Not during all those years while he grew up at the mission by the pearl-shell sea. And during the long afternoons in the schoolroom and the lonely nights, he would remember the campfire, and the family he had once known. He would remember his mother, and the touch of her skin, and her presence next to him. And he would wonder what had happened to them—for it was, as Liyan had said, too far to walk and he had no visitors.

Many years later, when John Jagamarra had grown to be a man and had a son of his own, they went back to Dryborough Station.

The place had long since been abandoned to the drought. The homestead was deserted. The stockyards were falling down and the water hole was dry. And down the overgrown track, only a few sheets of rusting tin were left to show that there had once been a camp under the acacia trees.

There was no one to tell them where the people had gone, or to say what had happened.

John Jagamarra camped under the trees and lit his fire where it had always been. He sang softly to himself and his son, trying to re-member the words that Jabal had used and their meanings. Remembering the story of Crow and the Eagle. Remembering the pain that lived inside him, and the sight of Liyan sprawled in the weeping dust. Telling these things to his boy.

That night, under the watching eyes of the stars, among the Ancestral spirits of the ancient land, John Jagamarra knew that he would look for his mother and those people to whom he belonged—and would keep on looking for them until they were found, no matter how many years it took.

And in the morning before they left, John Jagamarra gathered a handful of ashes and black charcoal from the fire, and rubbed it into his skin and into the flesh of his young son. He rubbed it in as deep as he could, so that it might become part of them and never wash out again. Not now. Not as long as they lived.